THE SINGING MAN

Adapted from a West African Folktale

by Angela Shelf Medearis
illustrated by Terea Shaffer

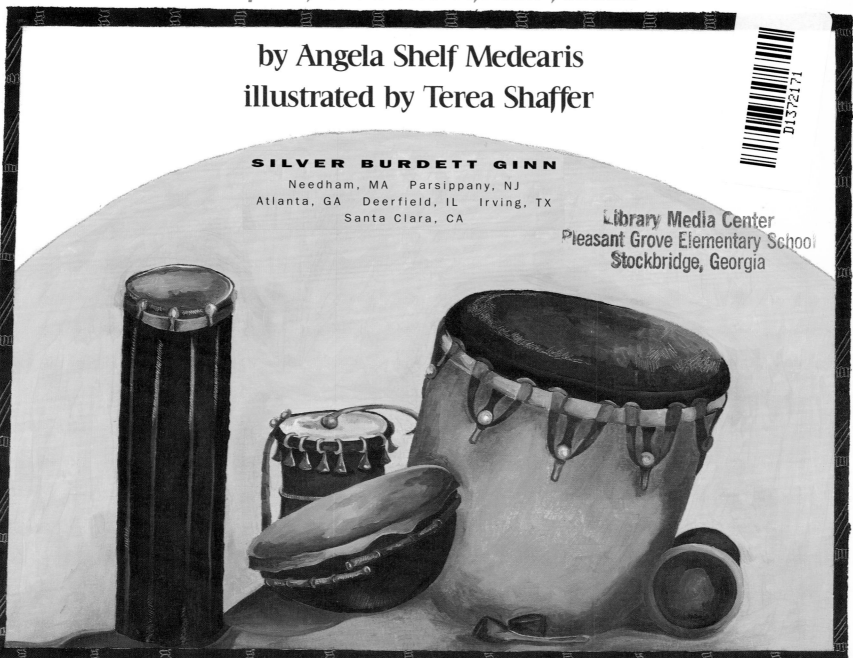

SILVER BURDETT GINN

Needham, MA   Parsippany, NJ
Atlanta, GA   Deerfield, IL   Irving, TX
Santa Clara, CA

For my musical brother, Howard L. Shelf, II, with love.

A.S.M.

For my sister, Tonya, for showing me what love and
courage really mean to my "little" sister, Lisha.
Thanks for the laughs. And to Wayne Skyers, because
I love you.

T.S.

SILVER BURDETT GINN
A Division of Simon & Schuster
160 Gould Street
Needham Heights, MA 02194–2310

Simon & Schuster edition, 1996

1 2 3 4 5 6 7 8 9 10 BA 01 00 99 98 97 96 95

ISBN 0–663–59271–2

The Singing Man is based on a folktale which is told by the Yoruba tribe in Nigeria.

In most African villages, those who made their living as *griots* or praise singers were viewed differently from ordinary musicians. The *griot* or praise singer was like a walking history book. The songs he sang traced the ancestors of the king or chief of the village, and hundreds of years of African history. These songs were passed from one praise singer to another for generations. The singer had a certain power over a king or chief because he could use his songs to either praise or condemn a chief's actions and decisions.

Praise singers and their songs helped to preserve the wonderful history of the African people. Long before African history was written in books, it was sung.

— *Angela Shelf Medearis*

I prepared the illustrations in this book using oil paints. I used a combination of oil paints and colored pencils for the borders. The colors were inspired by the textiles of West Africa. Through color, texture, and the characters portrayed, I wanted to show the diversity of Nigeria's people and landscapes.

— *Terea Shaffer*

Long ago in West Africa, the people spoke of the Singing Man. Some tell his story this way . . .

In a small village near the city of Lagos, there lived a man and woman who had three sons: Swanga, Taki, and Banzar.

When the boys of the village reached a certain age, their fathers took them deep into the bush for their manhood ceremony. The elders shared the wisdom of their years, and the young men danced and feasted with the boys. When the manhood ceremonies were over, the boys chose their life's work.

After Swanga was initiated into manhood, he decided to become a farmer and follow his father into the fields. The two men labored under the hot sun to grow acres of beans, grain, and yams.

When Taki was initiated, he decided to become a blacksmith. He fanned the flames of the fire and twisted the hot metal into tools. Then he took his wares to sell at the market.

But Banzar, the third brother, had no interest in these things. He did not want to be a farmer or a blacksmith. And he hated the very thought of selling things all day in the noisy, crowded marketplace.

Banzar loved music and nature. Every day he listened to the songs the birds sang, the tune that the wind whispered to the trees, and the melody the river made as it rushed over the rocks.

Soon it was time for Banzar to be initiated into manhood. After the secret ceremony, the elders of the village called Banzar before them. "What work will you do to help the village?" asked one of the elders.

"I want to be a musician," Banzar said.

"A musician!" said the elders. They whispered among themselves for a moment. Then they spoke quietly to Banzar's father.

"The elders say that music is not an acceptable choice," Banzar's father told his son. "Can music grow yams to fill your stomach? Can music make iron into tools to sell in the marketplace? The elders have declared that you must work for the good of the village or you cannot remain here. Please, son, make another choice. If you don't, you will have to leave. We must abide by the wisdom of the elders."

"I am sorry, Father," Banzar said. "I want only to be a musician, so I will go."

Banzar and his parents were very sad. When it was time for Banzar to leave, his father gave him a few coins. His mother gave him a water jug and a package of food. Banzar took their gifts and his flute. He waved goodbye to his family. Then he set off on the road to the town of Otolo.

Banzar walked for a long time. The birds chirped and a gentle breeze blew through the trees. He took out his flute and began to play. When he finished his song, he felt better and decided to eat. He sat down on a flat rock and unwrapped his food. As he started his meal, a blind man came down the road, swinging a crooked wooden stick in front of him. He wore the necklace of a praise singer and had an omele drum tied to his back. He played the drum when he sang praise songs for the village chiefs. For a few coins, he sang special songs he composed to honor the chiefs and his ancestors. He traveled from village to village, singing about the history of the African people.

"Good day to you, my father," said Banzar politely. "Have you eaten yet?"

"Good day to you, my son," said the old man. "Yes, I have eaten. Thank you very much. Could you tell me if I'm near the town of Otolo?"

"Yes, it is just down the road," said Banzar. "I'm going to Otolo also."

"Then we can travel together," said the old man. "Are you going to the marketplace to buy or to sell?"

"Neither," said Banzar. "I have just a few coins and therefore I cannot buy anything. The only thing I own is my flute, and I would never sell that."

"Ah," said the old man. "You must be a musician. Let me hear you play."

Banzar made the flute trill like a songbird.

"Yes, you have the gift," said the old man. "Why don't you travel with me? My name is Sholo. If you help me, I will teach you the ways of a musician."

"Thank you, Sholo," said Banzar. He finished his meal and together they traveled to Otolo.

"We will go to the chief's house," said Sholo as he placed his hand on Banzar's arm. "I will show you how to make your living as a musician."

Banzar and the old man turned up and down the narrow streets of Otolo and through the busy marketplace until they came to the chief's house.

Sholo squatted in front of the door. He placed the omele drum between his knees and beat out a wild rhythm. **PUM PUM BA LUM BO, PUM PUM BA LUM BO.** The old man sang of the mighty warriors of Otolo and of the chief's bravery in battle. He sang of the chief's goodness to his people and his wisdom as a leader. A crowd gathered around Sholo and Banzar. They clapped and danced to the music of the drum. The chief came out of his house and sat upon his chair. He listened solemnly to the old man's music.

Sholo sang and played for a long time. When he seemed to tire of singing, Banzar played his flute along with the **PUM PUM BA LUM BO** of the omele drum. He played the songs that he had learned from nature.

When the music stopped, the crowd clapped their hands. The chief gave Banzar and Sholo money and food and lodging for the night.

As they prepared their sleeping mats, Sholo told Banzar about the history of the praise singers.

For many years, Banzar traveled with Sholo from town to town. Sholo taught Banzar how to play the omele drum and compose the praise songs that honored the ancestors of the village chiefs. "We are the keepers of the past," Sholo told Banzar. "A people without a past have no future."

As the years went by, Banzar grew taller and stronger. But Sholo grew older and more feeble. It took longer and longer for them to travel from village to village. And then one day, Sholo died.

For a long time, Banzar stopped playing his flute. He sat by the river for hours, gently tapping Sholo's omele drum and thinking about his friend. He remembered Sholo's words.

"I alone know the history of our people," Banzar thought to himself. "I must tell them about the past so they will be strong in the future. I know that is what Sholo would want me to do."

Suddenly Banzar felt better. He lifted his flute to his lips and played song after song. He pounded out the **PUM PUM BA LUM BO** beat on the omele drum. He made up a song about Sholo and his wisdom. Then Banzar, the praise singer, picked up his instruments and traveled to the nearest town.

Banzar became very famous. When he entered a village, the children would clap their hands and shout, "The singing man has come! The singing man has come!" The children would dance before Banzar all the way to the house of the chief.

Now Banzar was the one who squatted down in front of the chief's door. He beat the wild **PUM PUM BA LUM BO, PUM PUM BA LUM BO** sound on the drum in the same way Sholo had for so many years.

Banzar made a very good living as a praise singer. But he was lonely. He missed Sholo. He thought often about his mother and father and his brothers, Swanga and Taki. He wondered if he would ever see his family again.

One day Banzar's travels brought him to the city of Lagos. The Feast of Igodo, the yam festival celebration, had begun. Everyone was rejoicing that the harvest season was over — with music, feasting, and dancing. All the praise singers had been invited to attend. One by one they played the omele drums and sang their songs for the king of Lagos. Each was given a small reward.

Finally it was Banzar's turn. He pounded out the wild **PUM PUM BA LUM BO, PUM PUM BA LUM BO** beat on his drum. He sang the songs of ancient Africa and the new songs he'd written about the king's wisdom, kindness, and bravery.

Then Banzar began to play his flute. He played the beautiful melodies that were taught him by the birds in the jungle. He trilled the secrets the wind whispered to the trees. He ended with the song the river sings on its journey to the sea.

When he finished playing, the king of Lagos beckoned him to come near. "Where did you learn our history, and to sing and play like that?" he asked.

"From Sholo, who is now dead," said Banzar.

"Of all the musicians I have heard, you have the greatest gift," said the king. "If you will remain in Lagos as my personal musician, you will be handsomely rewarded."

"I would be honored," said Banzar.

The king gave Banzar a house, money, and servants. Banzar wore robes made of rich material and a special golden necklace. He became a very respected man in Lagos.

One day, when Banzar was in the marketplace, he saw his brothers, Swanga and Taki. He greeted them, but they did not recognize him.

"How are your crops, friend?" asked Banzar.

"There has been a great famine in our land," said Swanga. "My fields barely yield anything to eat."

"How is your trade?" Banzar asked Taki.

"I have no money to buy iron," said Taki sadly. "Therefore I have nothing to make or to sell."

"Are your parents well?" asked Banzar.

"They live as well as can be expected in these hard times," said Swanga.

"Have you any other brothers?" asked Banzar.

"Our younger brother has been gone these many years," said Taki. "He would not work and desired only to play his flute. Can music make your fortune? So, he was sent away."

"I would like to visit with you at your home," said Banzar. "Tell your parents and your chief that the king's musician is coming."

Swanga and Taki left quickly to spread the news.

Banzar put on his finest robe. He filled his bags with food, gifts, and money, and called his servants. They went before Banzar into the village of his boyhood, beating drums and gongs and calling out, "Make way for the musician of the king of Lagos."

The procession stopped in front of the home of the village chief. The villagers gathered around Banzar. He sang song after song and beat out the wild **PUM PUM BA LUM BO, PUM PUM BA LUM BO** rhythm on his omele drum. The people clapped and clapped.

As the night drew near, Banzar saw his father, mother, and two brothers on the edge of the crowd. He took out his flute and stood before them. Then he played a few sad notes and sang:

A man and woman had three fine sons.
When the first son became a man, his desire was to
till the land,
When the second son became a man, his desire was to
make things of iron,
When the third son became a man, his desire was to
become a musician.
And the first son was honored,
and the second son was praised,
but the third son was cast out from his family to
wander for the rest of his days.

"Oh," said Banzar's father, "this song is just like the thing that has happened to us. Our third son wanted to be a musician. He has been gone these many years and by now is probably dead."

"No, my father, he lives," said Banzar. "I am he." Then Banzar and his family rejoiced. Banzar ordered his servants to prepare a feast. For many days, the village celebrated his good fortune. Banzar gave money and gifts to his family and the chief of the village. Then Banzar, the third son who became the king's musician, returned to the city of Lagos. Singing and dancing, his servants led the way.

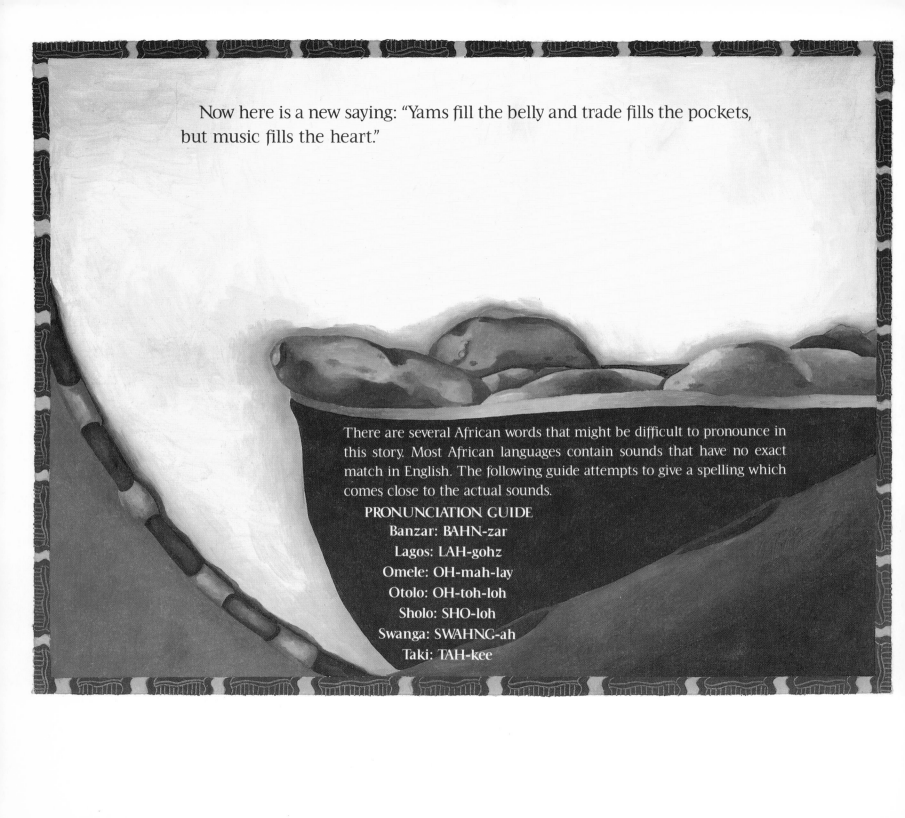

Now here is a new saying: "Yams fill the belly and trade fills the pockets, but music fills the heart."

There are several African words that might be difficult to pronounce in this story. Most African languages contain sounds that have no exact match in English. The following guide attempts to give a spelling which comes close to the actual sounds.

PRONUNCIATION GUIDE
Banzar: BAHN-zar
Lagos: LAH-gohz
Omele: OH-mah-lay
Otolo: OH-toh-loh
Sholo: SHO-loh
Swanga: SWAHNG-ah
Taki: TAH-kee

Glossary

a·bide by (ə bīd´ bī) *v.* To listen to and then follow what is said. *All the players abide by the rules.*

beck·on (bek´ n) *v.* To wave to someone to come closer. *They beckon to their father with their arms.*

bush (bush) *n.* Wild land as in the woods or in the jungle. *They are camping in the bush.*

fee·ble (fē´ bəl) *adj.* Not strong; weak. *The sick puppy gives a feeble cry when he sees his master.*

in·i·ti·ate (i nish´ ē āt) *v.* To take in as a member, often with a special ceremony. *Some clubs initiate new members only at certain times of the year.*